Magic Mischief!

Airy Fairy

Look out for more stories...

Magic Muddle!

This book belongs
to Takiya!!

Magic Mischief!

Margaret Ryan
illustrated by Teresa Murfin

■ SCHOLASTIC

To Sophie Jean Elizabeth
Love from Margaret Ryan

Scholastic Children's Books,
Commonwealth House, 1-19 New Oxford Street,
London, WC1A 1NU, UK
a division of Scholastic Ltd
London ~ New York ~ Toronto ~ Sydney ~ Auckland
Mexico City ~ New Delhi ~ Hong Kong

First published by Scholastic Ltd, 2003

ISBN 0 439 97849 1

Printed and bound by Cox and Wyman Ltd, Reading, Berks

2 4 6 8 10 9 7 5 3 1

Chapter One

It was school report day at Fairy
Gropplethorpe's Academy for Good Fairies,
and Airy Fairy's least favourite day of the year.

"My report's sure to be awful," she muttered
to her friends, Buttercup and Tingle. "I wish
we didn't get them just before the holidays."

"Perhaps it won't be as bad as you think,"
whispered Buttercup.

"Try not to worry about it," murmured Tingle.

"Do sit up straight and stop talking, Airy Fairy," frowned her teacher, Miss Stickler. "I never met such a girl for sprawling and muttering."

"Sorry, Miss Stickler," said Airy Fairy, and sat up straight and folded her arms.

"Now, pay attention, Fairies," said Miss Stickler, "while I read out your reports. Some of them are very very good." And she beamed at Scary Fairy, who was her niece, and always top of the class. "And some of them are very very bad." And she glared at Airy Fairy, who was always at the bottom.

Airy Fairy gave a huge sigh. It was always the same. Scary Fairy got everything right while she got everything wrong. It wasn't that she didn't try. It was just that things didn't work out somehow. Take last week, for instance. All the fairies were in the school hall preparing for the end of term concert. Everyone had a special job to do. Buttercup had magicked up the chairs, Tingle had magicked up the programmes, and Airy Fairy had been asked to magic up ten red coats for the school choir. But the spell went wrong when she sneezed in the middle, and she magicked up ten red goats instead. Ten badly behaved red goats.

They charged all round the hall, knocked over the chairs and ate the programmes. When Fairy Gropplethorpe arrived to magic them away, they biffed her on the behind and ate her wand. Then they knocked over Miss Stickler who was carrying a large vase full of flowers.

The vase and Miss Stickler crashed to the ground, and the goats galloped past them into the dining room, and polished off the school dinners. Then they trotted into the classroom and ate all the fairies' spelling books too. Airy Fairy didn't mind that. Her spelling was as dodgy as her magic.

But Fairy Gropplethorpe wasn't pleased, and Miss Stickler was furious about her best vase. Airy Fairy sighed just thinking about it. She didn't mean to cause trouble. It just seemed to follow her around.

She sighed again and looked out of the classroom window. A wintry sun shone on Fairy Gropplethorpe's Academy for Good Fairies and turned it to gold. To human beings the school just looked like an abandoned tree house, perched high up in an old oak, but it was home to ten tiny fairies.

"You are here to learn to do good fairy magic, Fairy Gropplethorpe had told them on their first day at school, "so that when you leave to go out into the world you can make it a better place. The humans have rather messed it up," she added sadly.

"You will also uphold the reputation of the school," said Miss Stickler, "as the very best in the country for good fairy magic. Is that clear?"

"Yes, Miss Stickler," all the fairies had chanted.

But some of them learned more quickly than others.

"Airy Fairy, will you stop looking out of the window and pay attention!"

"What? I mean, pardon? I mean, what did you say, Miss Stickler?"

"I said you haven't been listening to a word I've been saying. No wonder you're at the bottom of the class."

Scary Fairy, who sat behind Airy Fairy, giggled, and gave her a sly poke with her wand.

"Stupid. Stupid," she chanted.

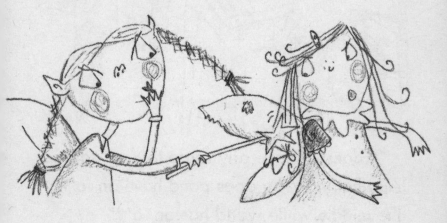

Miss Stickler picked up Airy Fairy's school report between finger and thumb and held it away from her.

"Just look at this report, Airy Fairy," she said. "Nothing out of ten for spelling."

"It doesn't make any sense to me," said Airy Fairy. "Why does pond have an 'o' in the middle while wand has an 'a'?"

"Nothing out of ten for magicking."

"The goats were a little mistake," said Airy Fairy. "It was an accident."

"Nothing out of ten for flying," went on Miss Stickler.

"I didn't see the window," said Airy Fairy. "I think all windows should have coloured glass in them, to let you know they're there. Or maybe have flowers painted on them. Pansies, I think. That would be nice. Or maybe I need glasses."

"Airy Fairy!" yelled Miss Stickler. "We are not talking about eyesight. We are talking about your school report."

"Yes, Miss Stickler. Sorry, Miss Stickler."

"A school report that is so awful Fairy Gropplethorpe wants to see you in her study right away."

"Oh no," gasped Buttercup and Tingle.

"Yes, Miss Stickler," sighed Airy Fairy, and trailed out to the front of the class.

On her way, she knocked over the table with the brushes and the paint pots.

"Oops, sorry," said Airy Fairy, and stopped to pick them up.

Scary Fairy pretended to help her.

"What an idiot you are," she whispered. "I bet Fairy Gropplethorpe gives you a terrible row. I bet she breaks your wand in two. She might even expel you!" And she gave Airy Fairy a sly nip.

Airy Fairy yelled and dropped a paint pot on Scary Fairy's toe.

"Do be careful, Airy Fairy," said Miss Stickler. "Scary Fairy's trying to help you. And pull up your socks and straighten your wings, and try to look like a fairy should. Dainty and pretty and TIDY."

"Yes, Miss Stickler," said Airy Fairy, and opened the classroom door.

"And don't bang the door."

"No, Miss Stickler," said Airy Fairy. But a gust of wind whistled along the corridor at that moment, and the classroom door banged shut and the handle fell off.

"Airy Fairy!" yelled Miss Stickler.

But Airy Fairy was too busy worrying about what Fairy Gropplethorpe would say to hear.

Airy Fairy made her way down the long corridor and the creaky flight of stairs to Fairy Gropplethorpe's study, and knocked on the door.

"Enter," boomed a voice.

Airy Fairy took a deep breath and went inside.

Fairy Gropplethorpe was sitting at a large desk in front of an open fire. An old dog lay warming himself on the hearth. Fairy Gropplethorpe had found him in a Christmas cracker years ago and had magicked him alive. He thumped his tail when he saw Airy Fairy.

"Hullo, Macduff," said Airy Fairy.

Macduff heaved himself on to his paws, knocked over the fire irons with his tail, and came to greet Airy Fairy. He licked her hands as she tickled behind his slightly singed ears.

Fairy Gropplethorpe shook her head.

"This is not a social call, Airy Fairy," she said. "I am concerned about your school report. It is not good."

"No, Fairy Gropplethorpe," sighed Airy Fairy, and stared at her pink fairy shoes. One of them had come undone so she bent down to fix it.

"Airy Fairy? Where are you? Where did you go? What ARE you doing?" said Fairy Gropplethorpe.

"Sorry," said Airy Fairy, and stood up quickly and bumped her head on Fairy Gropplethorpe's desk.

"Do try to pay attention, Airy Fairy," sighed Fairy Gropplethorpe. "And just look at the state of you. Your frock is grubby. Your knees are scraped. Your wings are bent and covered in sticking plaster. I suppose that happened in flying class."

Airy Fairy nodded and scuffed her toes on the carpet.

"A fairy must learn to LOOK where she's flying," said Fairy Gropplethorpe. "Not at everything else round about. She must learn to GLIDE through doorways. Not dive-bomb them. How you will cope with revolving doors when we do them next term I shudder to think."

Airy Fairy hung her head.

"Your magic class was a disaster too," Fairy Gropplethorpe added. "You got your spells wrong, didn't you?"

Airy Fairy nodded. "Sometimes I say a word wrong. Sometimes I spell a word wrong. And sometimes I just forget what I started out to do..."

Fairy Gropplethorpe shook her head.

"And I suppose you've bent your wand again."

Airy Fairy nodded once more.

"Let me see."

Airy Fairy held it out.

Fairy Gropplethorpe tutted.

"Wands should be straight, Airy Fairy,"
she said, taking it from her and fixing it.
"They should not be able to point round
corners. You've been poking people with it,
haven't you?"

Airy Fairy nodded again. Scary Fairy
always picked on her, and had poked her
first, but as usual, Airy Fairy had been the
one Miss Stickler had caught.

"Well," said Fairy Gropplethorpe. "I know it's almost the holidays, but this report is so bad that I'm afraid you leave me no choice. You will have to do some extra work before you can attend the school party on Christmas night. While all the other fairies are busy getting the hall ready you will go and spend some time as a tree fairy."

"Oh no," cried Airy Fairy. "Not a tree fairy. Not spend time on top of a prickly tree with pine needles sticking in my bottom! That's awful. I promise I'll do better in school, Fairy Gropplethorpe. I promise I'll try harder."

"Too late, Airy Fairy. I'm sorry, but you must learn to pay more attention in class. Now here is the address of the family you have to go to.

"Their name is Grimm, and they are grim in more ways than one. Most human beings try to be nicer to each other at this time of year, but not the Grimms. They will be a real test of your good fairy magic. If you have managed to learn any! You have six chances to try to improve the Grimms. Six spells to make them into nicer people before Christmas night. You will stand at the top of their Christmas tree and do your very best.

"I shall be keeping an eye on you, and, if you succeed, you can go to the party. If not, then I'm afraid you'll be in bed early. Do you understand?"

"Yes, Fairy Gropplethorpe," sighed Airy Fairy.

"Just try really hard, Airy Fairy," Fairy Gropplethorpe smiled. "I'm sure you can do it."

Airy Fairy trailed back to her class to tell Miss Stickler what Fairy Gropplethorpe had said.

"Well, perhaps this will teach you a lesson, Airy Fairy," said Miss Stickler. "Twenty-three Fairly Close isn't far away, but you'd better set off now, before it gets dark."

Airy Fairy turned to go.

"You can do the good fairy magic, Airy Fairy," said Tingle. "I know you can."

"Just remember the spells," said Buttercup. "You'll get to the party."

"I bet you won't," sneered Scary Fairy. Then she muttered to herself, "I'll make very sure of that."

Chapter Two

Airy Fairy set off for the Grimms', feeling miserable. "What a way to spend Christmas," she sighed. "It's bad enough being an orphaned fairy without being stuck up on top of a tree as well. Now where did I put that piece of paper with the address on it?"

She was so busy searching in her pockets and up her sleeves that she didn't see the big puddle by the side of the road.

And she certainly didn't see the big bus coming along.

WHOOSH! The bus went through the puddle. SPLOOSH! The water sprayed all over Airy Fairy.

"Oh no," she cried. "I'm soaked."

Water dripped from her hair, water dripped from her dress, water dripped from her nose.

She stood there shivering till a friendly cat gave her a ride on his back to twenty-three Fairly Close.

Airy Fairy blew a thank you into his ear and slid to the ground. She made her way to the front door, and let herself in through the bad-tempered letter box, which snapped shut on her fingers, and tore her pink fairy frock.

"Oh crumbs," said Airy Fairy. "Now everyone can see my pink knickers. I'll have to fix my frock." And she meant to do the spell for fixing frocks, but somehow it came out as the spell for stitching socks, and, when she looked, she had ten tiny socks stitched on the side of her fairy frock.

"Oh crumbs," said Airy Fairy again, and managed to do the spell to remove them. Then she looked around her at twenty-three Fairly Close. There was nobody home except for a cat and dog snoozing on the sofa, and a hamster who came out of his bed, filled his cheeks with peanuts, then went back to sleep.

"Right," said Airy Fairy. "I suppose I'd better get myself up on top of that Christmas tree."

The huge Christmas tree was standing at a drunken angle by the sitting room window. Its lower branches were covered in gold tinsel, its middle branches were covered in blue tinsel and its upper branches were covered in red tinsel. Only the spiky topmost branch was bare.

"Just waiting for me, I suppose," sighed Airy Fairy. "I wonder if my wings are working properly yet."

She took off from the orange and purple carpet, flew in a circle and ... missed the tree completely. DOINNNNG! She hit the window and slid down on to the ledge.

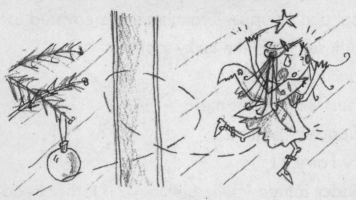

"Wings are still wonky then," she muttered. "Perhaps I should try taking off from the arm of that green chair. That should give me a bit of a lift."

She huffed and puffed up on to the arm of the chair and took off. Downwards.

She hit a football which carried her across the room and deposited her in the fireplace.

Soot fell down the chimney on to her head. Airy Fairy wiped her face with her frock.

"Could do better, Airy Fairy," she mimicked Miss Stickler's voice. "Perhaps if I climb up the curtain."

She huffed and puffed up the curtain, grabbed the curtain cord, and swung across like Tarzan.

Oouu-oouu-oo-ouch! She landed in the middle of the Christmas tree, in among the thickest, prickliest branches. She hit a shiny yellow bauble, slid down a spiky tinsel star and came to a halt on top of a wobbly red Santa who started to sing "We wish you a Merry Christmas," and gave her the fright of her life.

"I've a terrible feeling," she said, as she started the long climb up to the top of the tree, "that this isn't going to be a very merry Christmas at all."

Chapter Three

Airy Fairy had just got to the top of the tree when the family arrived home. She remembered to stand up straight and smile vacantly just in time.

Darren Grimm eyed her narrowly.

"I don't remember that tree fairy being there before we went out," he said.

"Course it was," said his twin sister, Dawn. "Don't you know anything? All Christmas trees have a fairy on the top."

"No, they don't," yelled Darren.

"Yes, they do," yelled Dawn.

"Be quiet, you two," said their mum, struggling in with the Christmas cake in one hand and a large turkey in the other.

"Give it a rest," said their grandma. "It's nearly Christmas."

"Can we open the presents under the tree then?" said Darren.

"No," said his mum.

"Not till tomorrow," said Dawn. "It's not Christmas till tomorrow. Don't you know anything."

"I know more than you, Clever-clogs."

"Stop it right now," yelled their mum. "Or Christmas will be cancelled. Darren, take the dog out for a walk. He's hopping about cross-legged."

"Not my turn," smirked Darren. "It's hers."

"It's not. It's his."

"It's not. I took him this morning."

"That was yesterday. *I* took him this morning."

"Liar liar, pants on fire!"

Airy Fairy watched in amazement as the twins pushed and poked at each other. Then she heard the dog give a deep sigh and lift his leg on the Christmas tree.

"I don't believe it," she muttered. "I know Fairy Gropplethorpe said the Grimms were grim, but this is awful."

"Now look what you've made the dog do," Mum yelled at the twins. "Get a mop and clean up that mess, Darren."

"It was her fault," said Darren.

"No, it wasn't. It was his fault," said Dawn.

"Oh dear," muttered Airy Fairy. "I think I'll have to use one of my six spells to fix this. I'll send Darren for a mop."

She made a magic circle with her wand, but, instead of saying "Darren Grimm mop up the mess," she got a little bit muddled and said, "Darren Grimm mess up the mop."

Darren grinned and rushed off to the kitchen. He came back with a mop and a large pair of scissors and gave the mop a haircut.

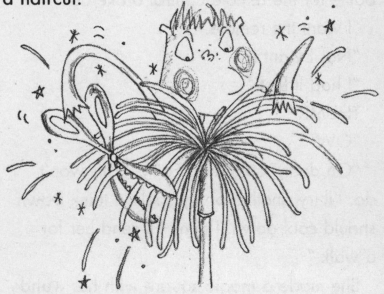

"What are you doing? Stop that this minute," yelled his mum. "That's my best mop."

"I need a cup of tea," said Grandma, and shuffled into the kitchen.

"Me too," muttered Dad. "Crazy kids!"

Airy Fairy shook her head. "Still nothing out of ten for spelling, Airy Fairy," she muttered.

It got worse.

The twins switched on the telly and the battle for the remote control broke out.

"I want the remote."

"No, I want it."

"I had it first."

THUMP.

"OW!"

"Oh dear," said Airy Fairy. "This won't do. I'll try another of my spells. I think Dawn should cool down. I think I'll send her for a walk."

She made a magic square with her wand and started writing in the air. But her spelling wasn't very good and, instead of sending Dawn for a walk she sent her for a wok.

Dawn disappeared into the kitchen and came back with a frying pan and a wooden spoon and clanged them together in everyone's ears.

"Oh dear," sighed Airy Fairy, trying to cover her own ears. "Still nothing out of ten for spelling, and I was sure I'd got that one right, too."

She was just going over the spell again in her head when a tiny movement at the window caught her eye. She looked over, and there was Scary Fairy making a horrible face at her. Airy Fairy got such a fright she nearly fell off the tree.

"Now what is she doing here?" she muttered. "She should be in school getting the hall ready for tonight's party. I bet she's come to cause more trouble."

She had. Scary Fairy wiggled her wand and suddenly Airy Fairy was covered in spots. Big red shiny spots, which itched.

It didn't take long for the Grimm family
to spot her.

"That tree fairy's got spots on her face,"
said Mum. "I don't remember them being
there before."

"I hope they're not catching," wheezed
Grandma. "I'm
an old lady.
I don't want
to catch any
horrible
diseases."

"I'll throw the fairy in the bin," said Dad,
and headed towards the tree.

"Oh no," Airy Fairy thought aloud. "I can't let them throw me in the bin. I'll never be able to do my good fairy magic if I'm in the bin. I must do a spell to stop them talking about me."

She made a magic figure of eight with her wand and she meant to say, "Please stop the Grimms talking," but she was still thinking about Dawn and said, "Please stop the Grimms walking."

"Hey, what's happened?" cried Dad, suddenly halting two feet from the tree. "My legs have gone funny. I can't move."

"Me neither," said Mum, trying to stand up.

"Or us," said the twins, falling over on to the carpet.

"Huh," said Grandma, not getting up from the sofa. "Serves you right. Now you know what it's like. I've had bad legs for years, but I didn't get any sympathy from you lot."

"Oh no," muttered Airy Fairy. "Now what have I done? I've made things even worse."

She was just having a worry nibble at her bottom lip when —

PING! The branch below her creaked and Fairy Gropplethorpe appeared in front of her. She looked at Airy Fairy and shook her head.

"You've used up three of your spells already, Airy Fairy," she said, "and the Grimms are no better. And look at you, covered in spots, though that's not your fault. I'll deal with that person later, and I'll help you out just this once."

And she whisked her wand in a zigzag fashion and removed the spots from Airy Fairy, and the memory of what had happened from the Grimms.

"Now concentrate, Airy Fairy," she whispered before she disappeared. "Remember you only have three spells left to do some good fairy magic to improve the Grimms – or no Christmas party!"

Chapter Four

Christmas morning came early in the Grimm house. Airy Fairy felt she had hardly gone to sleep when the sitting room door banged open and the twins, still in their pyjamas, charged in. Mum, Dad and Grandma followed more slowly, scratching and yawning. Darren and Dawn made straight for the Christmas tree. It shivered and shook as they grabbed their presents from underneath. Airy Fairy held on tight as they began ripping off the wrapping paper.

"Yuck, what horrible jumpers," muttered the twins, as they unwrapped stripy, multicoloured sweaters. "We wouldn't be seen dead in those!" And they dropped them on the floor among the wrapping paper.

Airy Fairy gulped and looked at Grandma. Her face was like a stormy thundercloud.

"Ungrateful little brats," she muttered. "It took me a long time to knit those jumpers, with the arthritis in my old fingers."

The twins just shrugged.

Mum and Dad picked up their present from Darren and Dawn and shook it.

"What do you think it is?" Mum asked Dad. "It doesn't look very interesting, and it's a very odd shape."

"Dunno," muttered Dad, and gave it a poke. "It feels a bit lumpy and bumpy."

Airy Fairy drew in her breath and looked at the twins. Their brows were lowered and their mouths were turned down.

"We made that for you in school," they said. "It's a bowl for keeping sweets in. It's made out of papier mâché, and it took us ages to tear the paper up into tiny bits."

"Really," yawned Mum and Dad.

Grandma poked at the family's present to her with her stick.

"That parcel's soft and squashy," she said. "I hope it's not another pair of pink bedsocks. You always buy me pink bedsocks. I've got millions of them. I asked for a giant box of soft-centred chocolates. Why don't you listen? Why didn't you buy me those!"

Airy Fairy looked all round the family. None of them were happy. Their faces were nearly as mean as Scary Fairy's.

Oh dear, she thought. *This isn't a very good start to Christmas. Everyone's supposed to be jolly at this time of year. Perhaps I could do a little spell to make them all say they were only joking about the presents. Perhaps they could say something nice.*

She waved her little wand in a magic diamond and wrote in the air, "Make the Grimms say something nice." And she was trying so hard to get it right that she didn't notice Scary Fairy at the window using her wand to rewrite the spell so that it said,

"Make the Grimms bring on some mice." And instead of the family saying something nice, they all yelled "MICE!" Suddenly, there were mice everywhere. On the carpet, on the table, on Grandma's head. She tried to fend them off with her stick. "Get off me. Get off!"

There were mice under the chairs, under the sofa, under Mum's feet. She did a funny little dance to avoid them. "Go away. Go away!"

The mice ran up the wall, up the curtains, up Dad's trouser leg. He went bananas! "Get down. Get down!"

The mice scurried over the dog, over the cat, over the hamster's cage. The dog barked and pranced about, the cat miaowed and jumped up on Mum, the hamster trembled, shot back into his bed and pulled the cotton wool in after him.

Everyone was yelling and screaming and leaping about. The presents were trampled, the Christmas tree was knocked over and Airy Fairy crashed to the floor.

"Help," she yelled, but nobody heard the tiny fairy voice amid all the din.

Airy Fairy struggled to her feet, parted the Christmas tree branches, and peeped out. What a mess! Then she caught sight of the face at the window, laughing fit to burst. Scary Fairy! This was all her doing! Scary Fairy made a horrible face at Airy Fairy and disappeared.

"Scary Fairy's up to her usual tricks," muttered Airy Fairy. "Now I'll have to use up another of my spells to get rid of the mice."

Airy Fairy made another magic diamond in the air and said, "Mice, mice, disappear. Your presence isn't wanted here." This time the spell worked, and the mice disappeared as quickly as they had come.

The Grimm family stopped yelling and jumping around and looked suspiciously at each other.

"There's something very strange going on here," they all muttered, as they righted the Christmas tree, and stuck Airy Fairy back on the top. "Where did all these mice come from? Who brought them into the house?"

Nobody owned up.

"Was it your idea of a joke?" Mum and Dad asked the twins. "Have you got a box full of mice somewhere?"

The twins shook their heads. "We don't like mice. Bet they belong to Grandma. Bet she brought them in to put in that terrible stew she makes."

"I think it was you two, you horrible little toads," said Grandma. "You did it just to scare the life out of a poor old woman." And she waved her stick at them.

The Grimm family glowered at each other. Airy Fairy sighed. "Help," she muttered. "I haven't managed to do any good fairy magic to improve the Grimm family. They're worse then ever. Scary Fairy is out to ruin my chances of getting to the school Christmas party, and I've only got one spell left. What am I going to do?"

Chapter Five

Airy Fairy stood at the top of the tree and thought and thought. How could she use the one spell that she had left to sort out Scary Fairy and the Grimms?

She was so busy thinking she hardly noticed when the Grimms sat down to lunch. She hardly noticed when the twins had a Brussel sprout battle. She hardly noticed when Grandma took out her teeth to chew her turkey.

She hardly noticed when Mum and Dad and the twins started to scoff a large box of soft-centred chocolates that should have been for Grandma.

But she did notice a little cord hanging by the side of the window.

"That's the cord I swung on earlier," she said. "I bet it closes the curtains. If I could just get over there and pull the curtains shut, Scary Fairy wouldn't be able to see in to do any of her mischief. Then, perhaps, I could try to do some good fairy magic with my last spell. But I mustn't be seen."

She waited and waited till it was getting dark.

Perhaps the Grimms will close the curtains themselves, she thought, but they didn't. They were too busy fighting about what to watch on TV.

"We want to watch the cartoons," said the twins.

"I want to watch a game show," said Mum.

"I want to watch some sport," said Dad.

"I want to watch an old movie," said Grandma.

While they were arguing Airy Fairy saw her chance. She slid down from the topmost spiky branch. "Ow, rotten pine needles!" she muttered, and tiptoed along the branch nearest the window. So far so good. She glanced back over her shoulder at the Grimms. They were slouched on the sofa. Darren was sucking his thumb, Dawn was fiddling with her hair, Mum and Dad were still cramming in chocolates faster than you could say "GREAT BIG GREEDY GUTS!", and Grandma was starting to snore.

Airy Fairy reached the end of the branch. It bent downwards slightly and a red shiny bauble slid off and bounced on the carpet. Airy Fairy froze and held her breath. But no one had noticed. She stretched out to grab the curtain cord, but it was just out of reach.

"I wonder if I should try out my wings again," she muttered. "I wonder if I could fly across."

But before she could take off a hand shot out and grabbed her.

"Stupid fairy's fallen off the top of the tree," Darren said, and plonked her back on the topmost spiky branch.

Oh no, Airy Fairy thought, standing there with a frozen smile on her face. *Now what am I going to do?*

She waited till the Grimms were all fighting over a board game.

"I want to be first to start," said Darren.

"No, me," said Dawn. "I'm twenty-five minutes older than you."

"Then we'll be first," smirked Mum and Dad. "We're twenty-five years older than you."

"Then I'll be first," cackled Grandma. "I'm the oldest of the lot of you." And she grabbed the dice and threw a six.

Airy Fairy saw her chance. She gritted her teeth and slid down the tree on her bottom till she reached the part where the branches were thickest.

"I'll just trek through this jungle till I reach the curtains," she gasped. But she parted a branch and – "We wish you a merry Christmas. We wish you a merry Christmas…" She had trodden on the wobbly red Santa.

"How did that happen?" said Dawn. "There's nobody near the tree." And she went over to look. She found Airy Fairy standing there with her smile stuck on, and pine needles sticking out of her hair and her frock.

"That stupid fairy's fallen off the top branch again," she said, plonking her back. "You would think she was alive and could go walkabout or something."

Airy Fairy stood there staring straight ahead, not daring to move.

"What am I going to do?" she worried. "What am I going to do?"

To make matters worse, the Christmas tree lights started to blink. On-off. On-off. On-off. Some Christmas tree lights are supposed to blink, but not the Grimms'.

"What's wrong with the lights?" said Darren, and came over to give the tree a shake.

Airy Fairy held on tight.

"Probably just need a thump," said Dawn, and gave the tree a bigger shake.

Airy Fairy held on tighter.

The lights went out and stayed out.

Darren and Dawn shook the tree till Airy Fairy's head was spinning and she was sure she was going to fall off. Then, out of the corner of her eye she caught sight of a little light outside the window. It came from the end of Scary Fairy's wand. She was heading this way.

Airy Fairy was desperate. But the shaking tree gave her an idea. When the tree swung nearest the curtain, she clung on with her knees, reached out and pulled the curtain cord with all her might. The curtains slid shut, and there was so much commotion with the tree, nobody noticed.

But Airy Fairy noticed the angry expression on Scary Fairy's face just as the curtains closed, and heard the tiny tapping as she banged furiously on the window with her wand.

"That's sorted you out," grinned Airy Fairy.

The twins finally gave up shaking the tree and started feeding mince pies to the dog. He was promptly sick over Grandma's slippers.

Grandma kicked off her slippers and they landed on the cat.

He ran up the curtains and sat quivering on top of the curtain pole.

Mum looked over at him and frowned.

"Who closed these curtains?" she said. "You know I like to be able to look out to see what the neighbours are up to."

Oh no, thought Airy Fairy. *She's going to open the curtains. Scary Fairy will be able to do her worst again, after all my hard work. I'll have to do my last spell right now.*

And she screwed up her eyes, waved her little wand in a double circle and said,

"Please allow the family Grimm
To let the Christmas spirit in.
Grandma, parents, sister, brother.
Make them kinder to each other."

Airy Fairy opened her eyes and looked round. Nothing happened. There was silence.

"Oh no, Airy Fairy," she groaned. "Nothing out of ten for magic again. I'll never get to the Christmas party now!"

Then a wonderful thing took place.

"On second thoughts," said Mum. "I think I'll leave the curtains closed. It's cosier that way. Now would you like some soft-centred chocolates, Grandma? I bought them for everybody."

"Put them into that nice bowl the twins made us for Christmas," said Dad. "Weren't they clever."

"But not as clever as Grandma knitting us these super sweaters," said the twins. "They'll be great for when we go skateboarding in the park."

"Oh, you wouldn't catch me skateboarding," laughed Grandma. "I'll keep my feet firmly on the ground in my new pink bedsocks."

Airy Fairy couldn't believe her ears. Her last spell had actually worked. The Grimms were being nice to each other.

She smiled happily to herself. "That's better, Airy Fairy," she said. "One out of ten for magic."

"Oh, more than that, Airy Fairy," said a voice, as a branch creaked behind her and Fairy Gropplethorpe appeared. "Much more than that. You did very well indeed, despite certain people trying to hinder you."

Airy Fairy smiled but said nothing.
Nobody likes a tell-tale.

"Now come along," said Fairy
Gropplethorpe. "Your job here is done. It's
time to go back to school and get ready for
the party." And she waved her wand and
whisked them both away.

Chapter Six

Fairy Gropplethorpe's Academy was ready for
the Christmas party. The fairies had been busy
all afternoon decorating the school hall.
Buttercup had painted glittering silver stars on
the windows, while Tingle had twisted shiny
silver string into garlands that wove their way
round the walls. Tiny bunches of miniature
holly sat in hazelnut-shell bowls on the window
ledges, and trails of ivy hung from the lights.

Airy Fairy stood at the hall doorway and gazed in amazement.

Buttercup and Tingle caught sight of her. "Hooray, you're back," they cried and ran to give her a hug.

"You've all worked so hard," said Airy Fairy. "The hall is beautiful."

"Well, most of us have worked hard," muttered Tingle. "Some people kept disappearing all afternoon." And she looked over at Scary Fairy who was scowling in a corner.

Airy Fairy said nothing.

"So what happened, Airy Fairy?" asked Buttercup. "How did you get on? Were the Grimms really awful?"

"They were," said Airy Fairy, "but I managed to do some good fairy magic in the end. Fairy Gropplethorpe was really pleased, so she brought me back in time for the party. We rode part of the way on a red squirrel. He was a handsome fellow and very polite. His red bushy tail tickled my cheek all the way home."

"Oh, red squirrels are my favourite," sighed Tingle.

Scary Fairy scowled even more when she heard this. Red squirrels were everybody's favourite.

The door of the hall opened and Miss Stickler came in, followed by Fairy Gropplethorpe and Macduff. Macduff panted over to greet Airy Fairy and rubbed his great head on her grubby pink frock.

"Hullo, Macduff," smiled Airy Fairy. "Why aren't you ready for the party?" And without thinking, she raised her little wand and magicked him up a handsome red collar with a silver bell.

"There," she said, fastening it on. "You look very smart."

"Which is more than can be said for you, Airy Fairy," said Miss Stickler. "You can't go to the party looking like that, and we're about to play the first game. Go upstairs and get changed right away."

Airy Fairy flew upstairs.

"Hooray," she cried. "My wings are working again." And she dived into her bedroom, caught her wings in the door, and bent them all over again.

"Oops!"

She splashed her face with water from the tap and changed into her favourite jeans and a T-shirt.

"Now I'm ready to party," she said, and sat on the bannister and slid all the way back down to the hall. It was a pity she'd forgotten the knob at the end of the bannister was missing.

It was a pity the fairies and Miss Stickler were all lined up for a game of musical bumps. It was a pity Airy Fairy crashed right into them and knocked them all over.

"Airy Fairy," yelled Miss Stickler. "What are you doing? I never met such a girl for messing things up. Get into line immediately."

"Yes, Miss Stickler," grinned Airy Fairy, and looked around. "But there are only nine of us here," she said. "Where's Scary Fairy? Isn't she playing this game too?"

"No," said Miss Stickler. "Fairy Gropplethorpe said since the Grimm family no longer had a fairy at the top of their tree someone else should go and be there. Scary Fairy very kindly volunteered. Wasn't that good of her? Especially since she seems to have mislaid her wand and can't do any fairy magic."

"Oh yes, it's very good of her," said Airy Fairy, and looked at Fairy Gropplethorpe.

Fairy Gropplethorpe looked back, and Airy Fairy was almost sure she gave her a wink.

Fairy Gropplethorpe switched on the music and started to dance. "Let's party, Fairies!" she said.

Airy Fairy grinned happily. "No problem, Fairy Gropplethorpe. I can get ten out of ten for that!"

Airy Fairy

Fairies are meant to be dainty
and pretty and tidy – but Airy Fairy
is the messiest fairy around!

Look out for the next book in this series!

Young Hippo
**Terrific stories, brilliant characters
and fantastic pictures – try one today!**

There are loads of fun books to choose from:

Jan Dean
The Horror of the Black Light
The Terror of the Fireworms

Alan MacDonald
The Great Brain Robbery
The Great Escape

GHOSTLY TALES

Penny Dolan
The Ghost of Able Mabel
The Spectre of Hairy Hector

Disastrous Dez

Mary Hooper
Mischief and Mayhem!
Spooks and Scares!

The Chills

Frank Rodgers
Head for Trouble!
Haunted Treasure!

Wallace and Wajid

Franzeska G. Ewart
Bugging Miss Bannigan